My Friend Angelmouse

by Rodney Peppé

It was the windiest day ever when Quilly met his friend Angelmouse for the first time. He was hanging out his washing, when suddenly something blew into his clothes.

"Why do you have to hang your washing up where anyone can fly into it?" complained a little voice.

The owner of the voice was a little mouse.

"But you can't fly!" complained Quilly as he picked up the washing.

"I've got wings," said the mouse, following him. "Just like you!"

"But mice don't have wings," said Quilly. He was **very** confused.

"Well, I have got wings," insisted the mouse. "I'm learning to be an angel, at Angel School."

Quilly had never even heard
of Angel School.

"That's where angels learn things.
I'm learning how to walk like a
proper angel," explained the mouse.

"But I'm not very good at that yet,"
he sighed. "I keep bumping into the
other angels!"

"At Angel School you learn to paint rainbows too,"
continued the mouse. "I'm not very good at that either!"

"My teacher was very upset when I painted a rainbow on his robe!" said the little mouse sadly.

"And most important of all," the mouse continued, "you try very hard to be good. But sometimes I'm just not good enough."

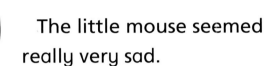

The little mouse seemed really very sad.

He explained to Quilly that today was the day he had to do his Angel Test.

"An Angel Test! What's that?" asked the bird.

"Well," said the mouse, "to see if you learned properly at Angel School, you are sent out to help someone."

"And that's called an Angel Test?" asked Quilly.
"Yes! And if you do it right," explained the mouse,
"you become a proper angel."

"Only, I lost my message with my instructions," said the little mouse. "So I don't know who to help. And if I don't help the right person…"

"...I'll never become an angel. They might even take my wings away."

"I'm sure we can find someone who needs help, Mouse," said Quilly. "Come on!"

Quilly and the mouse flew around the village, looking for someone to help.

But in the village shop, Little Petal and Hutchkin were already helping each other.

Elliemum and Baby Ellie were playing a game.

They didn't need any help.

And neither did Spencer.

Suddenly, Oswald came speeding towards them.

"No brakes! No brakes!"

he screamed.

"Doesn't **he** need helping?" asked the mouse.

"No, that's Oswald," said Quilly. "He's always like that."

"Oh if I don't help someone today," said the mouse, "I'll never be an angel."

Just then, the wind started to blow and blow and blow. A huge gust picked up Quilly and the mouse and blew them around wildly.

"**Help!**" cried Quilly.

"**Help!**" cried the mouse.

"Help!" cried Quilly again. He was being blown towards a windmill with whirling sails.

The mouse saw what was going to happen to Quilly if he didn't help him. So he flapped his wings and braced his ears, and grabbed the bird by his leg.

"Thank you, Mouse," said Quilly.
"You saved me!"
   Quilly began to stare at the mouse.
Something was shining above his head.
   "What's that over your head?"
Quilly asked.
   "It's a… you know… a thingamajig,"
said the mouse.
"Like angels have… a halo."

"Look," said Quilly. "There's a message…"

" …It says: **To pass your Angel Test, you must go and help a bird called Quilly**."

"That's the message I lost," said the mouse. "I'd better find this Quilly bird as quick as I can."

"But I'm Quilly, silly," said Quilly laughing. Then another message floated down.

Quilly read the second note.

"It says: **Congratulations. You have passed your Angel Test**. Does that mean you're an angel, Mouse?"

"Yes, that's what I am – Angelmouse," said Angelmouse.

"A real Angelmouse! With a thingamajig!"

The letter also said that Angelmouse was to stay in the village and help people whenever he was sent a message.

And that's how the little mouse became Quilly's best friend, Angelmouse.